Lindsey

by Chryssa
Atkinson

American Girl

For Jim, Sydney, and Sam; special thanks to
Andrea Weiss and her brilliant red pen

Published by Pleasant Company Publications
Text copyright © 2001 by Pleasant Company
Cover and story illustration copyright © 2001 by Zelda Bean
Back matter illustration copyright © 2001 by Tracy McGuinness
Printed in China
07 08 C&C 10 9 8 7

The illustrator would like to thank the wonderful Caitlin Rose Ward, model and inspira-
tion for the Lindsey illustrations.

Library of Congress Cataloging-in-Publication Data
Atkinson, Chryssa.
Lindsey / by Chryssa Atkinson.
p. cm. "American Girl Today."
Summary: Ten-year-old Lindsey is continually getting into trouble despite her well-
meaning, impulsive efforts to rescue a classmate from bullies, cheer up her depressed
uncle, help with her brother's bar mitzvah, brighten up her neighborhood, and spark a
romance between two teachers.
ISBN 1-58485-450-2
[1. Family life–Fiction. 2. Interpersonal relationships–Fiction.] I Title.
PZ7.A8636 Li 2001   [Fic]–dc21   2001036282

Contents

1

Over the Line

As soon as I saw the matzo ball sailing across the room, I tried to duck. But I didn't move fast enough. It hit me in the face, slid down the front of my brand-new dress, and landed on Mr. Tiny.

If you don't know what a matzo ball is, I'll tell you. It's a slippery, dumpling-like blob of mush that floats around in chicken soup. My dad says someday I'll learn to appreciate matzo balls. I don't think so.

Mr. Tiny is my dog, and he likes matzo balls. As soon as the flying one rolled off his back and hit the floor, he gobbled it up and wagged his tail. I, on the other hand, started crying. I'd completely ruined one of the most important days in my family's life.

I, Lindsey Bergman, deserved to get hit with a hundred flying matzo balls.

Most of my problems started a month ago, when I wrecked my school's pet parade. Kids spend months getting ready for the pet parade every year. It's a huge deal. They make overalls for their dogs and ballerina outfits for their hamsters—and that, my friend, is the problem. HAMSTERS SHOULD NOT WEAR BALLERINA OUTFITS!

At first I tried reasoning with my classmates. I passed out anti–pet parade fliers the week before, but nobody paid any attention to them. And my teacher, Miss Kinney, wouldn't let me give my "Down With Pets in Pants!" speech to the class. So I had to take drastic measures.

On parade day it was hot and sticky, and I knew that the animals must have been very uncomfortable. Have you ever *seen* an iguana in pants? It's just not right. So when I spotted Josh Thompson (total, TOTAL creep) dragging his iguana around in that cowboy outfit, I had to do something. I had to save at least one pet from complete humiliation.

I hid behind a bush, and when Josh came by, pulling his iguana in a wagon, I jumped out, grabbed the iguana, climbed the nearest tree, and refused to come down. OK, so the iguana didn't seem too happy. But it was for his own good.

Pretty soon everyone started screaming and yelling at me. Mr. Nelson, the principal, came running over and barked, "Get down now, Miss Bergman!" But I just closed my eyes and stayed right where I was.

Finally Mr. Nelson shouted that the parade was over and sent everyone back to their classrooms. There was a lot of complaining. I felt sorry for ruining everyone's fun, but I was sure it was the right thing to do.

Mr. Nelson took me to his office and made me sit in a sticky plastic chair while he gave me a lecture. Then he called Miss Kinney to come get me, and she marched me back to class.

When we got there, everyone stared at me the way you stare at an overcooked piece of asparagus that your mom is trying to make you eat. I actually thought I saw one kid's lip curling. I gave a feeble sort of really-sorry-for-ruining-your-fun smile, but they all just glared at me.

I tried to concentrate on Miss Kinney. She was announcing the Perfect World Collage assignment, which is the greatest assignment of the year. Everybody in the whole school does it—every grade. We can use any kind of stuff we want, and we glue it all onto a big piece of poster board to show what our perfect world would be like. Then the best collage from each grade is chosen for a special display in the library. How cool is that?

But it was hard for me to get too excited, because I could feel everyone's angry eyeballs burning a hole through the back of my head.

The rest of the school day was pretty quiet. I had a long, lonely scooter ride home. Except for when Josh

Thompson threw an empty milk carton at me.

It didn't get any better when I got home, either. Mom met me at the door with her own version of the asparagus face. Even my dog, Mr. Tiny, the most loyal and fabulous wiener dog in the history of the world, lowered his tail and slunk down to the basement at the sight of me.

My mom stared at me with one squinty eye. "Mr. Nelson called," she said. "Now, I want you to think very carefully before you answer me, Lindsey. WHAT WERE YOU THINKING? And don't say animal rights or world peace or saving the planet." Mom took a deep breath, paced around the living room a little, and then slumped into a chair. "You could have broken your neck."

"Um, I just remembered, I forgot to feed Mr. Tiny this morning," I squeaked and tried to make a run for the kitchen.

"Sit!" she said.

I sat.

Then I said, "I don't know. It just seemed like the right thing to do. The animals looked so unhappy, especially that little iguana. He was wearing pants and a hat, and he kept scratching at his belt buckle, and—"

"Enough, Lindsey. Go to your room. And while you're up there, I want you to write Josh Thompson an apology for terrorizing his iguana."

Was she kidding? Apologize to Josh Thompson? I'd rather eat thumbtacks.

"I really didn't need this today, Lindsey," Mom went on. "I've got enough to think about already." She sighed and rubbed her forehead. "We have some unusual family business to discuss at dinner tonight." Then she closed her eyes and pointed her finger toward the stairs.

I lowered my head. (You should always do this when you get in trouble. It makes your parents feel really bad, and they usually stop short of some really evil punishment.) I started to fold up my scooter, and that's when I noticed the little mud clods from the wheels all over the carpet. Oh, great.

"The scooter, Lindsey. Hand it over."

"No—not my scooter!" I protested. "Anything but my scooter! I'll eat liver! I'll eat the mud clods! I'll sing my apology to Josh over the loudspeaker at school! Just don't take my scooter!" I begged.

But my pleas fell on deaf ears (obviously the head-lowering thing hadn't worked). So I handed over my beloved scooter.

As luck would have it, my brother, Ethan (also known as Weasel Boy), chose that moment to come flying through the front door. "Hey, Mom! You're not going to believe what Lindsey did at school today! Henry told me that his little brother told him that Lindsey stole an iguana from some kid and—"

"We know, Ethan. It's been taken care of. Thank you for your report," Mom said.

Ethan grinned his most weasel-like grin right at me. "Man, if it weren't for Lindsey getting in trouble every five minutes, I'd have nothing to live for."

Let me tell you something about my brother. When you look up the word *annoying* in the dictionary, there's a big picture of Ethan. He's wearing his baseball cap backward and smiling his I'm-so-cool-I-can-hardly-believe-it smile, and his green and purple braces are full of popcorn husks and gummy worms. Do you get the picture?

I spotted one of Mr. Tiny's squeaky toys on the floor and threw it right at Ethan's annoying head.

"Cease fire," said my mom. "Lindsey, go to your room. Ethan, come into the kitchen with me. We have to pick out bar mitzvah invitations. I found some really sweet ones that I want to show you."

"*Sweet?* I'm becoming a man, Mom, not a candy cane," Ethan snorted.

A bar mitzvah is a Jewish ceremony that boys go through when they turn thirteen. They have to prepare for it by learning lots of Hebrew and studying the Torah, and when they're all done, they're men — at least according to Jewish custom, that is. If you knew my brother, you'd know that sometimes they just let kids through to be nice.

"If you're becoming a man," I yelled as I stomped up the stairs, "I'm Miss America!"

I slammed the door to my room, flopped onto my bed, opened my laptop, and flicked it on. Instead of writing Josh an apology, I started one of my lists. I make lists when my brain is in a frazzle and I have trouble sorting things out.

Here's how the list went:

Stuff I should have thought of before I decided to wreck the pet parade:

1. Maybe Josh's iguana just looked unhappy. That might have been his favorite hat. I might have caused permanent emotional damage.

2. Josh will definitely do something rotten to get back at me (like the time he stuffed a peach into my trumpet when I was playing "Jingle Bells," and it cost me $15 of my own allowance to have it removed).

3. Mom and Dad are going to be giving me the asparagus look for days.

4. I'm banished to my room, and I'll probably never see my scooter again as long as I live. Woe is me.

Mr. Tiny was scratching at my door, so I let him in. Then he chewed on my freshly printed list while I started my apology note to Josh.

It went something like . . .

. . . blah, blah, blah, I'm so very sorry if I scared your iguana. I love animals and would never want to hurt them. I only meant to stop an evil act. Please forgive me, and ask your iguana to do the same.

Sincerely,
Lindsey

I printed out the note and stuffed it in my book bag. Then I took out my trumpet and started playing "Taps" as loud as I could. Mr. Tiny ran under the bed.

I played until my lips got all numb and fuzzy. It was getting dark, and I was feeling really sorry for myself. Why couldn't things have gone differently? If everyone had read my fabulous anti–pet parade flyers and had decided—like reasonable people—that the parade was awful, I might have been a hero. They might have elected me class president. I might have been on the news. I might have been named honorary spokesperson for the Humane Society . . . Hey, was that my stomach growling?

I was so hungry that I was about to eat the Cheerios off an art project I made in first grade, when I heard Dad coming up the stairs. I can always tell his sound from everyone else's.

Dad has long, skinny insect legs that kind of glide instead of stomp. (I'm a stomper. I take after Mom's side of the family.) Besides the gliding, Dad's always got a lot of junk rattling in his pockets—spare change, little gadgets, stuff he finds in between the car seats. My dad is an engineer at a high-tech science lab. He has to wear a special ID tag and get buzzed into his building at work. To put it simply: he's a geek. Anyway, I knew it was Dad. *Jangle, jangle, clink, glide.* He knocked on my door, using our secret knock. Maybe he wasn't as mad as Mom.

"Who goes there?" I said in my most pathetic you-can-stop-punishing-me-now-because-I'm-really-sorry voice.

"He Who Must Be Obeyed," Dad said. He was trying to be funny. That was good.

"Come in," I answered, trying to look pale.

He sat down on the bed next to me, took off his glasses, and rubbed his nose.

"Lindsey, Lindsey, Lindsey," he sighed.

"Dad, Dad, Dad," I sighed back.

"Lindsey, this is the third time this year we've had a call from Mr. Nelson—"

"I know, Dad, but this time it wasn't my fault," I blurted. "I had to do something. Animals' lives were at stake!"

"Lindsey, you and I both know that there were no lives at stake this afternoon," he scolded. "You simply decided to take matters into your own hands without considering the consequences." Dad chewed thoughtfully on the end of his glasses. "There's a fine line between helping and meddling, Lindsey, and today you were on the wrong side of that line."

"But how am I supposed to know which side is which? I thought helping animals was on the right side." This was not making a lot of sense to me.

"You weren't helping anyone or anything when you put yourself and Josh's pet in danger. It was wrong to take that iguana hostage. Before you jump into things, you need to think about how your actions might affect other people."

"But that's so much thinking!" I protested. "I'm much better at doing stuff than thinking about it."

"Well, my dear," he said, "a week without your scooter will give you a little more time to work on your thinking. By the way, your mother wanted to take your laptop away, too, but I convinced her it served an educational purpose."

"Gee, thanks," I mumbled. But I really was grateful. I couldn't survive a week without both my laptop *and* my scooter. "You know," I added, trying for a little sympathy, "I'll probably get blisters all over my feet from walking the thirty miles to school."

"It's about six blocks, and I think you'll live." Then, without the teensiest bit of pity, Dad stood up and beckoned me with a long, bony finger. "Come downstairs for dinner. Your mother and I have something we need to discuss with you and Ethan."

What could they possibly have to discuss?

When we got downstairs, Mom and Ethan were already sitting at the table. (It was spaghetti night. Yum! Things were looking up.) Ethan sneered at me, but Mom was just muttering to herself and smearing big blobs of butter on her French bread. That's when I knew something major was going on. Mom is not the muttering, buttering type.

Dad and I sat down, and no one said anything for a while. We just watched Mom with the butter. Ethan was picking the black olives out of his spaghetti sauce and flicking them onto his placemat. I completely lost my appetite. Brothers.

Dad cleared his throat a couple of times. "Kids," he started. He took a deep breath and stared out into space. "Sometimes families go through changes. Now, changes can be good. They can also be challenging. Remember when Lindsey first got Mr. Tiny, and he wasn't housebroken, and we had to leave newspaper all over the house, and sometimes, well, sometimes we stepped in little accidents . . . ?" Dad's voice trailed off. He'd been twirling a huge bunch of spaghetti on his fork, and now it was about the size of a tennis ball.

Finally Mom reached over with her fork and

started stabbing at the spaghetti ball till it fell apart. Dad made a little yelping noise.

Ethan shot a look at me, and for two seconds we were on the same team. Our parents had lost their minds, and we were going to have to take care of them. Ethan and I nodded bravely to each other.

Dad grabbed the fork from Mom and went on. "A new situation has come up that is not exactly like a new pet coming into one's life but is almost like it, except for the newspaper—"

"Oh, for goodness sake, Gordy," Mom broke in, "just spit it out."

"You're right, honey," Dad said. "Kids, your uncle Bernie is coming to live with us."

Ethan let out a scream, tipped his chair over backward, and started rolling around on the floor, howling, "Noooooooooooo!"

Mom put her head in her hands and began to hum a tuneless song. Dad got up, stepped over Ethan, and went to the kitchen to pour himself a cup of coffee.

All I could manage to do was croak out, "For how long?"

Mom picked up her head. "For as long as it takes." Then she shot Ethan the evil eye. He stopped rolling.

First of all, let me say that Uncle Bernie is my favorite uncle. But he's also kind of like a big, sticky, grumpy bear—the kind of bear you might not want around the house every day sitting on your furniture and stuff. I guess that's what Aunt Rhonda thought, too, because about six months ago, she told Uncle Bernie that she wanted a divorce. She took all her clothes and anything else that she didn't want to get sticky stuff all over, and she left.

"Your dad went to Uncle Bernie's this afternoon to check on him," Mom explained, "and he found Uncle Bernie on the couch in his pajamas, watching soap operas and dipping cheese puffs into chunky peanut butter. Dad got worried. People shouldn't live on junk food and wear pajamas all day."

Personally, I didn't think that sounded so bad.

Pajamas are really comfortable.

"This can't be happening!" Ethan moaned. "This is going to be totally embarrassing! I'll never be able to have friends over again. Don't you remember the time he came here when we were on vacation and mowed the lawn in his boxer shorts? Mrs. Schumacher actually called the police!"

Dad came back with his coffee. "Ethan, Lindsey. Families have to stick together. Uncle Bernie is family, so we're going to stick with him."

"Yeah," Ethan snorted, "and he'll be sticking to the sofa cushions!"

OK, so Uncle Bernie is kind of a mess, I thought. But he's our mess. "I think it'll be fun to have Uncle Bernie here," I said, trying to sound as helpful as possible. (Maybe they'd reconsider the scooter thing if they saw how unselfish I was being.)

Ethan groaned.

"Well, OK," I admitted. "Maybe it won't be exactly fun, but it will be interesting."

"That's the spirit, honey," said Dad.

That night before bed, I made a list of stuff that might cheer up Uncle Bernie:

1. Decorate the spare bedroom with balloons and crepe paper and pictures of All-Star Wrestlers (he loves those guys).

2. Teach Mr. Tiny to carry a "Welcome, Our Dear Favorite Uncle Bernie!" sign in his teeth.

3. Find a helmet that will fit Uncle Bernie, and teach him how to ride my scooter (if I ever get it back).

4. Make sure Mom buys some cheese puffs and extra peanut butter.

It's always good to have a plan.

2

A Great Day

I did get blisters on my feet from walking the thirty miles (OK, six blocks) to and from school, but I'd made it through seven days without my scooter. I deserved an award.

It was Friday after band practice, and I was putting Band-Aids on my feet when my band teacher, Mr. Pingler, asked me to stay after and have a chat. I figured he was going to congratulate me on my progress. I'd been practicing like crazy lately, and I was sure it showed.

"Well, you certainly do enjoy playing the trumpet, don't you, Lindsey," Mr. Pingler said.

I knew he'd noticed! "Yes, Mr. Pingler. I think it's

the most wonderful instrument in the world. It's shiny
and loud and happy-sounding—"

"Yes, it is loud, isn't it?" He looked kind of tired.
"Perhaps we could work on that. Maybe you could
hold back just a bit during practice so we can hear
some of the less shiny, happy-sounding instruments,"
he said. He smiled a painful-looking smile.

I knew that smile. It was the same one that Mom
had used at the neighborhood meeting the week
before, when she got stuck talking to Mrs. Schumacher
about her zinnia fungus.

Mr. Pingler looked really down in the dumps. His
shirt was halfway untucked, and his pants were all
wrinkled. Plus, they were way too short. I could see
that he was wearing one blue sock and one black one.
Maybe he's sick, I thought. Come to think of it, I did
see him take some aspirin during practice.

"Are you feeling OK, Mr. Pingler?" I asked.

"Oh, I'm fine, Lindsey," he said.

"Did you eat lunch today, Mr. Pingler? Because

lunch is a very important meal. It really gets you through the afternoon."

"Come to think of it, no," he answered. "I didn't have any lunch today."

"Ah-ha! There you go," I said.

He smiled a real smile this time. "There you go. I'll see you next week, Lindsey."

I turned to leave, but suddenly a giant lightbulb popped on in my head. Maybe Mr. Pingler was lonely! I knew he wasn't married. "Um, Mr. Pingler," I said, "do you have a girlfriend?"

He made a choking, snorting sound. "Lindsey, why don't you concentrate on your trumpet, and I'll try to remember to eat lunch tomorrow, OK?"

"OK, Mr. Pingler. See you next week."

Walking home, I couldn't stop thinking about Mr. Pingler. He was really skinny, and he didn't have anyone to take care of him. What if he didn't even have pets for company? What if he skipped dinner, too? I didn't want him to end up like Uncle Bernie—surviving on cheese puffs and peanut butter.

Mr. Pingler needed romance in his life. Romance always made people want to eat better and wear nicer clothes. But who would want to be romantic with Mr. Pingler? (I didn't want to think about that part too much.)

I was plotting how to get Mr. Pingler a girlfriend and trying not to step on any cracks in the sidewalk, when I heard a loud scream. I looked up and saw Blair Kolinski and Missy Rizzo (the two biggest bullies in my class) standing under a tree and laughing like hyenas. Someone's legs were hanging out of the tree.

I crept behind a bush and peered up. The legs belonged to April Greely. Her backpack was dangling from another branch, higher up. Apparently April was not a champion tree climber. She was starting to lose her grip on the branch.

Blair and Missy thought it was hilarious. "Hey, April," said Blair, "how's the air up there? It's really stinky down here, because all we can smell are your FEET!" Then she and Missy grabbed April's shoes right off her feet and ran.

I came out from behind the bush. April let go of the branch and came down with a thud. Her face was all streaky from crying, and she was muttering something about how she was so lame, she couldn't even climb a stupid tree. Then she started crying again.

I told her it was OK and that lots of people had trouble with trees. I pretended not to notice the crying too much. "Do you want me to get your backpack for you?" I asked.

She nodded.

I climbed up and got the backpack. On the way down, I ripped my tights.

"They've been doing that to me all week," said April. "They throw my backpack into a tree, take my shoes, and stuff them into the trash can at the park."

"Well, at least you know where to find your shoes," I offered.

"Yeah," she said. "So, do you want to walk home together?"

"Um, yeah, sure." I secretly hoped that no one would see us, though. April wasn't the most popular girl at school. In fact, she was kind of the opposite. Aside from not being very coordinated, April had this habit of blowing spit bubbles. Maybe she didn't know it, but blowing spit bubbles around a bunch of fourth graders looking for someone to pick on is not really a good plan.

We stopped by the park, and April fished her shoes out of the garbage can. "Gross," she said as she shook someone's half-eaten sandwich off them.

"Yeah, trash cans are disgusting. They're almost as bad as my brother's bedroom. I try not to dig around in *there* too often, either," I said.

April laughed.

We managed to make it all the way to my house without anyone noticing us. The big surprise for me was that April was pretty fun to walk home with. She did a great impression of Mr. Nelson yelling at me, where she held her breath and squinched her face so that it got all red, and she looked just like him. I laughed so hard, I almost swallowed my tongue.

When we got to my door, April looked like she wanted me to invite her in. I panicked and told her that my Uncle Bernie had just moved in and that he was sort of bizarre and I couldn't have anyone in the house. I felt bad about lying, but I had to work up to being brave about hanging out with April.

She didn't seem too mad and said that she understood about weird relatives. Then she said, "Lindsey, what you did at the pet parade was really brave. I'd never have the guts to do something like that."

I sort of shrugged.

"See you tomorrow at school," she said.

"Bye, April," I said, and I watched her walk down the sidewalk. As she turned the corner, I saw her blow a huge spit bubble. In some parts of the world, I thought, that might be considered a talent.

What was wrong with me? What did I care if Blair and Missy and everyone else saw me with April? April was nice. April was funny. April thought I was brave! Tomorrow I was going to ask April over. Well, maybe the day after tomorrow.

I started to open our front door. Then I stopped and took a deep breath. Uncle Bernie was going to be in there. He had moved in earlier in the day while Ethan and I were at school, and I was supposed to hang out with him while Mom and Ethan were out doing bar mitzvah stuff.

I peeked through the living-room window. Uncle Bernie was in there, all right. I saw a crumpled cheese-puff bag on the coffee table. And as I looked more closely, I thought I saw his feet hanging over the edge of the sofa. They were either feet or two giant loaves of French bread.

I counted to three and walked through the door. "Where's my favorite uncle?" I called in my cheeriest favorite-niece voice.

"Lying in here with a lousy stomach ache," came the reply.

This wasn't going to be easy.

It turned out that those *were* his feet hanging over the couch. They were attached to the rest of him, which was wearing plaid pants and a Hawaiian shirt that was buttoned all wonky. And he had an ice pack on his head.

"Hey, I thought you said you had a stomach ache," I said, pointing to the ice pack.

"Lindsey, Lindsey, you're young. The young never understand. First it's the stomach, then it's the head, then—*echh,* I shouldn't bother you with my problems." He patted my hand.

"Come on, Uncle Bernie," I said, "let's get some fresh air." I grabbed his hand and tried to pull him up.

He wouldn't budge.

I pulled again. Finally I managed to haul him into a sitting position. "Stay right there while I find your shoes, OK?"

I ran down to the guest room to get his white patent leather loafers. I guess he'd liked the wrestling posters I put up because he had already moved one from the closet door to right over his bed. I noticed, too, that he hadn't bothered to unpack like a normal person. Instead of putting his stuff in the drawers that we'd cleared out for him, he'd just dumped his things out of his suitcases onto the floor. Mom was going to go ballistic.

I'd have to worry about that later, though. I had to get Uncle Bernie off that couch before he made it his permanent home.

I found one shoe under his bed and the other one in the bathroom. By the time I got back upstairs, he was snoring.

"Uncle Bernie, let's go!"

He sputtered as I yanked him off the couch and crammed his shoes on his feet.

"It's time for your scooter lesson!" I said.

"Scooter lesson? Pumpkin, I don't think I'm up for

anything like that," he protested, veering back toward the couch.

"Even for your favorite niece?" I begged. I grabbed my scooter from the hall, brushed off the dust, and gave it a big kiss. "I haven't been able to use this baby for an entire week, Uncle Bernie, but I'm willing to let you take the first ride."

He rolled his eyes and took my hand. "How could I possibly refuse such generosity." Then he motioned to Mr. Tiny, who was waiting by the door. "Come on, boy, this ought to be a good show."

Everything went fine—at first. I had strapped my helmet onto Uncle Bernie's head. The helmet was a little small and made him look like a giant Hawaiian Q-Tip, but it was better than nothing. He was laughing and whooping and screaming "YEEE-HAAA!" in no time, zipping up and down the sidewalk. Some of the neighbors even came out to watch.

I was feeling very proud of myself. Mom and Dad were going to be totally amazed. Uncle Bernie hadn't moved this fast since, well, I didn't think I'd ever seen Uncle Bernie move this fast.

He was zooming back and forth, with Mr. Tiny chasing after him and wagging his tail and barking. Suddenly Mr. Tiny spotted a rabbit and took off. He darted right in front of Uncle Bernie, who swerved and did this sort of gigantic flip over the Thompsons' fence. He landed in the middle of Mrs. Thompson's rosebushes.

Mrs. Thompson came running out of the house in her aerobics outfit. "You lunatic!" she yelled. "You're a grown man, for heaven's sake— what on earth are you doing riding a child's toy up and down the street like a crazy person?"

"Believe me," said Uncle Bernie, who was still lying on his back, wincing in pain from the thorns, "this crazy person will not be visiting your rose-bushes again."

"I should hope not," said Mrs. Thompson. Uncle Bernie sat up slowly and started examining his body for puncture wounds.

Mrs. Thompson examined her bushes.

"I'll be happy to pay for any damages," offered Uncle Bernie.

"That won't be necessary. These are very hardy plants. As for you, Lindsey, please keep that dog on a leash." She looked at her watch. "You've made me miss three minutes of my workout tape. I hate having to rewind it."

"Sorry, Mrs. Thompson," I said as she headed back toward the house.

Mr. Tiny, who had returned from his rabbit chase, was snuffling around our ankles. I picked him up and pretended to scold him. (I can never actually scold him for real—he's way too cute.)

"I'm going home now," said Uncle Bernie as he limped over the fence and down the sidewalk. He was still wearing my helmet, and there were leaves and twigs stuck in his clothes and a big rip in his pants. I felt terrible.

"What a dork," I heard a snotty voice say. "Where did he get that outfit, a costume store?" I whipped around, and there was Josh Thompson.

"He's my uncle, and he's not a dork. He's a hundred times cooler than you'll ever be, you iguana torturer," I said. Mr. Tiny growled a little.

"You'd better take your stupid dog and get off our property," said Josh. "Geez, Bergman, you can't stay out of trouble, can you?"

I wasn't sure why Josh hated me so much. Aside from taking his iguana, I'd never done anything to him. But he was always a creep to me. He must not have appreciated that apology note I'd left in his locker. I'd even drawn an iguana on it.

"Joshy!" Mrs. Thompson yelled from their front door. She was jogging in place and doing little kicks. "You get in here and clean up that pigsty of a room, pronto!"

"Yeah, JOSHY, you'd better get in there," I said, stifling a giggle.

Josh turned to go. Then he looked back at me with his beady little eyes. "If you say one word to anyone about my mom calling me 'Joshy,' you are dead meat."

I just smiled at him, picked up my scooter, and started home.

"I mean it!" he yelled.

I pretended not to hear.

Back in the house, Uncle Bernie was dabbing at his puncture wounds with some antiseptic. Mom and Ethan were hovering over him.

"Wow," said Ethan, "I didn't know rosebushes had teeth."

"They don't have teeth, Weasel Breath. They have thorns," I answered, trotting to my uncle's side. "Uncle Bernie was very brave. You should have seen him tearing it up on my scooter!"

Between winces, Uncle Bernie grinned sheepishly. "I did tear it up a little, didn't I, Pumpkin?"

"I think Uncle Bernie has had enough 'tearing it up' for a while, Lindsey," my mother said sternly. Then she marched me up to my room for a lecture

on the difference between helping Uncle Bernie
versus helping Uncle Bernie break his neck. (Ethan
loved it. I could hear him breathing on the other side
of the door.)

"Lindsey, I know you were trying to cheer up
your uncle, and I appreciate that. But I wish you
would learn to think things through before you dive
into them headfirst. By the way, would you mind
explaining to me how you managed to tear your
brand-new tights?"

I was about to tell her all about saving April,
when Ethan toppled into my room. He'd been leaning
on the door a little too hard with his big, fat head.

"Oops," he said.

Mom grabbed him by the arm. "Come on, nosy,
we have to look at the catering menus for your bar
mitzvah. It's only four weeks away, you know!"

What was wrong with these people? All they
seemed to care about was Ethan's stupid bar mitzvah.
No one cared about what I had achieved today.

I whipped open my laptop and made a list of the day's accomplishments:

1. Saved April from tree. Found out she's really funny. Maybe we could hang out together. I'll try to get over spit-bubble thing.

2. Learned Mr. Pingler doesn't have a girlfriend. Must make plan for finding him a suitable date.

3. Got Uncle Bernie off couch and onto scooter. Aunt Rhonda lived with Uncle Bernie for twenty-five years, and she never got him off the couch!

4. Found out Josh's mother calls him "Joshy." Sure to come in handy someday.

That night, I was feeling so good about myself that I didn't even mind sitting through the torture of Mom, Dad, and Ethan arguing about the bar mitzvah. Ethan wanted to invite every girl in the eighth grade (like they'd actually come) and have glow-in-the-dark

invitations and some rock band called the Twisted
Turtles. Mom was pleading for good taste, and Dad
was rattling on about how the spiritual importance of
the bar mitzvah should not be overshadowed by the
material trappings of the party.

Uncle Bernie was asleep on the sofa with a half-
eaten Hershey bar in his hand.

Now, that was the right idea.

3

What a Mess!

It was Monday, and I was zooming along at top speed on my scooter so I wouldn't be late for school. I couldn't wait to tell Miss Kinney how I was doing on my Perfect World Collage.

I'd spent all day Sunday looking through a gazillion magazines for pictures to cut out. Do you know how hard it is to find really good pictures of dachshunds and trumpets? I was also going to draw and paint some stuff and use some of Mr. Tiny's fur (that was going to be tricky) for a special part in the middle. It was going to be spectacular.

The kindergartners usually glued food all over their collages, and the sixth-grade girls put photos of themselves next to movie stars so it looked like they were kissing (blech!). The boys always did ones where they were world-famous sports heroes and got to eat pizza every day. I was sure that my collage was going to be the fourth-grade winner.

I was imagining what I was going to say in my interview for the newspaper . . . "Miss Bergman, how did you ever come up with the idea for that cute little heart made out of dog hair?" . . . when I heard a very familiar sound.

"You guys! Those are brand-new shoes. My mom's going to kill me!"

I came to a screeching halt. Blair and Missy had April Greely dangling from a tree again, and they were pulling her shoes off her feet.

I'm not sure what came over me, but I let out a huge Tarzan yell and ran up behind Blair, grabbed hold of her, and pulled. She came down on top of me, and April came down on top of her. Missy just stood there watching with her mouth hanging open.

"Get off me, you cow!" Blair yelled at April.

"Hey, I could say the same to you!" I yelled at Blair, which was really hard because I had two people on top of me. When we all got untangled and stood up, I could tell that Blair was really mad. Her face was all purple, and her usually perfect hair was a mess.

"You guys are so dead," she said, pointing to April and me with a perfectly polished sparkle-blue fingernail.

"Yeah," said Missy. (As far as I could tell, Missy wasn't too smart. I'd never heard her use a word with more than one syllable.)

"Why are *we* dead?" I asked. "You're the ones torturing innocent people."

"What we do is none of your business," Blair shot back. "But then, you don't know much about minding your own business, do you? You pet-parade wrecker."

I started to lunge at her, but April grabbed onto my book bag. "Oh, how cute," Blair sneered. "The freaks are looking out for each other."

"Yeah," said Missy.

"Well, freaks," Blair said, "you'd *better* be looking out for each other, because now I'm going to be looking for *you*."

"Yeah," said Missy.

Then Blair floofed her hair and grabbed Missy's arm, and the two of them pranced away.

I looked at April. April looked at me. And we started laughing hysterically. We laughed the rest of the way to school. The fact that Blair was probably going to kill us didn't matter. For the moment, we'd won, and April's new shoes hadn't ended up in the garbage can.

"You know, that's the second time you've saved my life," said April. "I don't know how I'm going to repay you."

"How about coming over after school today and helping me torture my brother?" I said.

"Really? Seriously? Yeah, sure, OK!" she sputtered. I thought she was going to pass out, she looked so excited. Then she caught her breath. "But what about your bizarre uncle?"

"Oh, he's not that bad. He's bizarre in a good way."

"Yeah, I have a cousin like that," April said, smiling.

I had a feeling that being friends with her was going to be pretty fun.

My happy feeling didn't last too long, though, because the minute we got to class, Miss Kinney called me up to the front of the room. Blair was standing next to her. Blair's hair looked a lot worse than before, and somehow she'd gotten mud all over her clothes. She was sniffling and whimpering.

"Lindsey," said Miss Kinney, "Blair says that you attacked her on the way to school. Now, I have no idea why you would do such a thing, but you will be staying after school to discuss this incident with me."

I couldn't believe what I was hearing. "But Miss Kinney, I—"

"That's enough, Lindsey. Now take your seat. We'll discuss it after school."

I walked to my seat and tried not to scream. As I passed Missy's desk, she gave me an evil grin. Her hands were caked with mud. I should have known those two would concoct an evil plan to ruin my life. My parents were going to kill me when they found out I was in trouble *again*. Even worse, they were probably going to take my scooter away—AGAIN. I was doomed.

During lunch, I stared into space while April ate my tuna sandwich. During math, I stared out the window. During language arts, I stared at my workbook.

When the last bell finally rang, everyone scrambled for the door. On her way past, April gave my arm a little squeeze. I attempted a brave smile and slumped down in my seat.

After the room had cleared out, Miss Kinney came over and sat down next to me. "OK, Lindsey, why don't you tell me your version of what happened," she said, handing me a wedge from the orange that she was peeling.

I was starving, so I stuffed the wedge in my mouth and told her the whole story, starting with the first time I'd seen Blair and Missy take April's shoes.

Miss Kinney must have believed me, because she patted my knee and gave me the rest of her orange. Then she asked me if I'd like to help her change the bulletin boards and get them ready for the Perfect World Collages.

"Your wish is my command," I said. I loved hanging out with Miss Kinney.

While she went to get some background paper and a staple remover, I wandered over to her desk and sat in her chair. Now, my desk at home was pretty messy, but it was nothing compared to Miss Kinney's. Her desk was a disaster. There were stacks of books and magazines and piles of papers everywhere. How could she find anything in that clutter?

What Miss Kinney needed was a little organization. I scooped all the papers together and started sorting them, using my own personal, top-secret filing system: wrinkled or extra-large stuff in one pile, lined papers in another pile, and plain-paper projects in another pile. I used construction paper for dividers, and I even rearranged all of her sticky notes so that they looked like a rainbow—first pink, then yellow, then green, then blue . . . it looked really pretty.

Miss Kinney was taking a long time finding that staple remover, so I went to work on the books and magazines, stacking them according to size.

I was arranging the last pile when I found a gold mine—a magazine opened to a page with a quiz on it. The quiz was called, "What's Your Type? Pick the Man for You," and Miss Kinney had filled it out.

I read the quiz and saw that she had checked off "sporty," "good cook," "romantic," and "funny."

This was great. It was better than great! The answer to helping Mr. Pingler with his love life was right in front of me.

Miss Kinney would be perfect for Mr. Pingler. He wasn't exactly sporty, but he might be romantic, and anyone could learn how to cook. And Miss Kinney was friendly and smart and very understanding about things like dorky clothes. She also loved music, and Mr. Pingler was the band teacher. It was perfect. All I had to do was figure out how to get them together.

Just then Miss Kinney came back. "Sorry that took me so long, Lindsey," she said. "Mr. Nelson needed to speak to me about something, and—WHAT HAVE YOU DONE TO MY DESK?"

I stuffed the magazine back into the pile and beamed. "I gave you my special Lindsey Bergman Cleaning and Organizing Service for absolutely no charge! Doesn't it look great? And I've made these special piles so you'll be able to find everything really fast . . . Are you all right, Miss Kinney?" She was sitting in a chair with her head in her hands. "Do you want me to go get the nurse?"

"I'm fine, Lindsey," she said through her fingers. She lifted her head and looked at me. "Please don't ever touch the things on my desk again. I already have a system—or *had* one—and now I'll have to spend the rest of the afternoon . . . oh, never mind."

"I'm sorry, Miss Kinney."

"I know." She sighed. "I think you'd better go now."

"But what about helping you with the bulletin board?" I asked.

"I think you've helped enough for one day."

"Please don't call my parents, Miss Kinney. I can't take another week without my scooter. Plus, there was this thing with my uncle and some rosebushes and—"

"I won't call them, Lindsey. But promise me you'll never touch my desk again."

"I promise and pinky-swear," I said, offering her my little finger.

"Pinky-swear," she said, linking hers with mine.

Then I picked up my book bag and got out of there as fast as I could. Miss Kinney looked like she might cry, and I'd already used her last tissue.

When I got out into the hall, April was still waiting for me. "Wow, you didn't have to stay," I said, but secretly I was pleased that she had.

"Oh, that's OK," she replied, working on a spit bubble. "I was practicing." She was getting really good, too. Her bubble was about the size of a golf ball. "Do you have any gum?" she asked.

"Nope," I said, "but I've got something better." I told her about finding the quiz on Miss Kinney's desk, and about my matchmaking plan. "You and I have a job to do, April. We have to get Miss Kinney to fall in love with Mr. Pingler."

"No way," April said. "They're way too old for that. They've gotta be at least thirty!"

"April, if we set our minds to it, we can do anything." I took her arm, and we marched out of the school building together.

When we got to my house, we went around to the back door and practically tripped over Uncle Bernie, who had his head inside a trash can. He was making an awful moaning noise. My mother was sitting on the back stoop, watching him with her eyebrows up.

April gave me a funny look. "Let me guess," she whispered. "This is your uncle."

I nodded. "Um, Uncle Bernie, what are you doing digging around in that trash?"

Mom said, "Honey, Uncle Bernie did something by accident this morning. Maybe he'll take his head out of the garbage can and tell you about it." She looked at Uncle Bernie. Uncle Bernie didn't move.

Mom cleared her throat and told me that Uncle Bernie had decided to help out around the house that morning. He'd vacuumed and dusted and thrown out a pile of paper clippings that he'd found on the dining-room floor.

Paper clippings? Dining-room floor? I screamed, "Those were my Perfect World Collage pictures!"

Now I knew how Miss Kinney felt.

Finally Uncle Bernie pulled his head out of the garbage can. He looked miserable, and his hair was standing up funny. "They're ruined, Pumpkin. I'm sorry," he said.

"WHAT? But the collage is due tomorrow!" Now I knew how it felt to feel even *worse* than Miss Kinney. At least nobody threw her stuff in the trash. "I'll never make it," I moaned.

"I could help," offered April. "I'm already done with my collage."

"Smart girl," said Uncle Bernie, perking up. "Who is this girl? I like this girl." He put his arm around April. She beamed. Then he said, "I'll help, too."

So we all went inside to start cutting out more magazine pictures. Mom made popcorn to fortify us.

April ended up staying for dinner. She got to see the entire crazy Bergman family in action. Dad played with his calculator and separated his food so nothing was touching. Ethan chewed with his mouth open and pretended his fork was an electric guitar, and Mom dunked her bread in her soup and stirred it around.

Uncle Bernie told stories about when he and Dad were kids. The best one was about Wilbur Funt, the neighborhood bully who used to beat up Dad and

Uncle Bernie for wearing plaid pants. I wondered if Wilbur Funt was related to Blair or Missy.

Dad walked April home after dinner, and Uncle Bernie and I finished putting my collage together in the basement. We even got Mr. Tiny to give up some of his tummy fur to make a little fur heart for the center of the collage.

It looked awesome. I glued lots of dog pictures around the fur heart, and I put a shiny trumpet in each corner. I drew a bunch of math problems inside a giant trash can (where all math problems belong). I also drew a picture of myself zooming through my world on a bright blue, motorized scooter. I painted peace signs and happy faces to show that everyone would get along in my world, and, across the bottom, I drew pictures of kids showing grownups how to do things like climb trees and play hopscotch. I even taped a string of little colored lightbulbs around the border so that when you plugged it in, it looked like an advertisement for a movie.

While Uncle Bernie and I were cleaning up, we heard Mom and Ethan upstairs arguing about—you guessed it—the bar mitzvah. Ethan was bragging about how much money he was going to get from everyone, and Mom was telling him not to be greedy. She also announced that there was no way she was going to pay a thousand dollars for a band called the Twisted Turtles. This did not go over well with Ethan. We heard a door slam.

"I remember my bar mitzvah," said Uncle Bernie, looking up at the ceiling and shaking his head. "It wasn't fancy like this thing your parents are planning for Ethan, but it was a very special day."

"Did you have a live band?" I asked.

"Not unless you count my great-aunt Mildred and her accordion," he snorted. "My ears rang for a week!"

I was getting ready for bed that night when I realized April and I hadn't had any time to work on our Miss Kinney and Mr. Pingler plan. I grabbed my laptop, crawled into bed, and pulled the covers over my head so my parents wouldn't see any light coming from my room. They're sticklers about bedtime.

Secret Plan for Fixing Up
Miss Kinney and Mr. Pingler

1. Mention to Mr. Pingler that Miss Kinney thinks he's a wonderful band teacher.

2. Mention to Miss Kinney that Mr. Pingler thinks she's the best fourth-grade teacher in the school.

3. Learn more about what kind of food Miss Kinney likes, and then find out if Mr. Pingler can cook it.

4. Bring a men's fashion magazine to school and show Mr. Pingler a few outfits that might look good on him.

5. Watch for signs of mad crush, and then figure out what to do next.

Now I could sleep.

4

A Not-So-Perfect World

The next morning, Mom was throwing cushions off the couch because she was late for her water aerobics class and couldn't find her floaties. The batteries in my dad's calculator had gone out in the middle of some major equation, and he was having a fit. Ethan was hiding in the bathroom, applying an entire tube of zit cream. The pressure of practicing Hebrew every night had finally gotten to him, and his face had broken out like a pepperoni pizza.

I was sitting on the kitchen floor brushing Mr. Tiny when the phone rang. It rang about ten times before Uncle Bernie finally put down the comics, got up, and answered it.

It was his ex-wife—my ex-aunt—Aunt Rhonda. She had called to inform us that she was bringing her new boyfriend to Ethan's bar mitzvah.

Uncle Bernie slammed down the phone and threw his bowl of oatmeal across the breakfast room. Then he started jumping up and down like a crazy person. Dad and Mom came running.

They tried to calm him down, but he just kept yelling, "That woman is evil, pure evil!" Mom gave him a paper bag to breathe into.

Mr. Tiny trotted into the breakfast room and started licking oatmeal off the wall just as Ethan ran out of the bathroom. His face was all white and crusty.

I noticed my camera on the counter and knew that a picture of crusty-faced Ethan would give me ammunition for weeks, but this was one mess I did not want to get in the middle of. "What kind of a family is this?" I yelled. "Can't any of you act normal?"

I put away the dog brush, grabbed my Perfect World Collage, and made a run for it.

I met April at the corner and told her all about my flying-oatmeal, goop-faced-brother, crazy-family morning. I knew she would understand. She actually thought my family was fun and exciting. I knew they were insane.

April's collage was almost as big as mine, and we couldn't see where we were going. We were having a great time bumping into each other like big, goofy sailboats when suddenly Blair and Missy jumped out of the bushes in front of us.

Not again, I thought. But it was even worse than usual, because Josh Thompson jumped out with them. They were now a terrible team of three. April and I were doomed.

"Look at the two dorky ducks waddling to school on their big webbed feet!" taunted Blair.

"Yeah," said Missy.

"Yeah," said Josh.

I grabbed April's arm and said "QUACK!" and flashed them all a big duck smile. Then we turned on our heels and left them standing there speechless while we waddled down the street.

"Waddle, waddle!" yelled Blair.

"Yeah!" yelled Missy and Josh.

"Bye, JOSHY!" I shouted over my shoulder.

"Joshy?" said Blair. Josh glared at me like he wanted to break my arm.

April and I waddled away as fast as our webbed feet would carry us.

As soon as we got to school and had turned in our collages, I mentioned to Miss Kinney that Mr. Pingler thought she was a really great teacher. She looked at me kind of funny, but I figured she was still mad about my organizing her desk.

"Really, Miss Kinney," I insisted, "he said that he admires you."

April nodded in agreement.

Miss Kinney looked suspicious. "Would you girls take your seats, please," she said. "Oh, and by the way,

Lindsey, would you mind telling me where I might find my little red grading notebook?"

"Sure," I said, "it's in the lined-paper pile because of those grid pages, and it's under the red sheet of construction paper, because it's red. It's totally obvious if you just think it through. Oh, and he thinks you're brilliant," I added.

"Who?" Miss Kinney asked.

"Mr. Pingler!" I said.

Miss Kinney's eyes narrowed. "Lindsey, please sit down." She was trying to look serious, but I could tell she was impressed. For the rest of the day, I winked at her a lot.

At band practice that afternoon, I told Mr. Pingler that Miss Kinney had told our whole class what a great band teacher he was.

"Really?" said Mr. Pingler, raising one eyebrow. "Well, that's very flattering, Lindsey."

"She said you have a wonderful way with the

students, and that you're very stylish."

"Stylish?" he asked. He was blushing!

"Absolutely, Mr. Pingler," I lied. I normally don't like lying, but this was for a good cause. I made the lie a little bigger by telling him that Miss Kinney really wanted him to come to our class to give a special lecture on jazz music, since he was such an expert.

"That's quite a compliment," he said. "Do you really think the students would enjoy a talk about jazz music?"

"Sure they would, Mr. Pingler. They love jazz, and you're so good at talking." Actually, I didn't know exactly what jazz was, and I didn't think anyone else in the fourth grade did either. But it didn't matter—everybody always fell asleep no matter what he was talking about. I just needed to get him into our class.

"Well, I suppose I could discuss the possibility with Miss Kinney—"

"Maybe you'd better wait," I interrupted. "I think she wants to mention it to you first."

Whew, I thought. I'd have to corner Miss Kinney tomorrow and make her think that my great idea was *her* great idea. "See you later, Mr. Pingler!" I chirped as I grabbed my trumpet and headed for the door.

Have you ever noticed how really ugly most trash cans are? They're grubby, puke-green, and depressing. Just because they're full of trash is no reason for them to be ugly. At least that's what April and I thought as we were walking down my street on Tuesday afternoon and saw all my neighbors dragging their trash cans down to the curb. There wasn't a happy-looking one in the bunch (trash can *or* neighbor).

"Too bad you can't paint them or put stickers on them or something," said April.

"That's it, April!" I shouted. "You're brilliant! My mom's got a bunch of smiley-face stickers down in the basement, from when she was a Brownie leader. We can stick them on every garbage can on the block and really liven up the whole street!"

When we got to my house, Uncle Bernie was on the couch with a bag of cheese puffs, watching Spanish television. He was still in his pajamas.

"Hey, Uncle Bernie," I said in my cheeriest favorite-niece voice, "are you feeling any better?"

He grunted.

"Uncle Bernie," said April (she'd started calling him "Uncle," which was cute), "would you like to help Lindsey and me? We're going to make all the trash cans look nice."

"Nice, schmice," he grumbled. "What's the point? Trash cans are for trash. They're trashy. They should look trashy."

Until that phone call from Aunt Rhonda, he had really seemed to be improving. "Oh, cheer up, Uncle Bernie," I said. "I bet Aunt Rhonda's new boyfriend has yellow teeth and really bad breath."

He just closed his eyes and snorted.

It was going to take a lot of work to straighten him out, but right now April and I had garbage to deal with. We went down to the basement and found the smiley-face stickers without too much trouble. They were crammed into a big box labeled "Brownie Troop Junk." Next to the label, my mom had drawn a big skull and crossbones that said KEEP OUT. I'm sure she meant Ethan. We dug right in.

"Boy, Uncle Bernie seems really depressed," April said as we unpacked the box.

"Yeah," I said, "I think my uncle is a little like these stickers. He's sort of dusty and crumpled, but if you stuck him in the right place, he'd be really useful. Right now, he's stuck on the couch."

"I know what you mean," said April. "I've felt dusty and crumpled before, too."

We grabbed an armload of stickers and headed back outside. By then, almost everyone's trash cans were lined up at the curb. We got to work, and when we finished, the street was full of happy, smiling trash cans. The garbage collectors were going to love it.

April and I admired our handiwork and gave

each other a big high-five. Then April went home for dinner, and I went home to deal with Uncle Bernie and hear the latest bar mitzvah update. (Oy.)

I didn't make too much progress with Uncle Bernie, other than getting him to wash his pajamas, but it was a start. For all the talk about our family working together to help him, it seemed like I was doing most of the work.

At dinner, I tried to tell everyone about the trash-can decorating project. I kept clinking my water glass and clearing my throat, but Dad was busy punching numbers into his recharged calculator, Uncle Bernie was pushing food around on his plate, and Mom and Ethan were sorting note cards and arguing over the bar mitzvah guest list.

There was an "A" pile for the important guests, a "B" pile for sort-of important guests, and a "C" pile for people nobody liked but who'd have hissy-fits if they weren't invited. Aunt Rhonda fit into this last category.

In the interest of family peace, I volunteered to

address bar mitzvah invitations. After dinner, I took
the piles and my mom's address book and headed
upstairs.

While I was working, I happened to notice that
my cousin Sophie (actually my first-cousin-once-
removed) on my mom's side had been left off the
invitation list. It was obviously a mistake, since all our
other cousins were invited, so I added her to the pile.

I suddenly got a brilliant idea. Sophie was pretty
and nice and just a little younger than Uncle Bernie.
They'd be perfect for each other! I addressed an invitation for her and wrote a note that said, "Looking
forward to seeing you!"

I was a genius.

Sophie would meet Uncle Bernie and think he
was totally charming, and Uncle Bernie would be so
flattered that he'd forget all about evil Aunt Rhonda.
He might even ask Sophie to dance. Of course, Uncle
Bernie dancing is like a hose going all wacky when
you turn it on full blast and let go of it, but, hey,

maybe Sophie would think it was cute. I couldn't wait to find out.

Before bed, I practiced my trumpet and, just for Mr. Pingler, tried not to sound too loud and shiny. As I was playing, I happened to look out my bedroom window, and guess what I saw? A whole street full of GLOWING happy faces! I had no idea those stickers were glow-in-the-dark. How cool is that?

There was someone out there, too, holding a flashlight. It was our nosy neighbor, Mrs. Schumacher. She was pacing up and down the street, studying the trash cans very carefully.

The next morning, I made Uncle Bernie's oatmeal, unplugged the TV, and dashed for the door. Dad was working crazy hours on a new project, and Mom was neck-deep in Ethan's bar mitzvah, so once again it was up to me to make sure that Uncle Bernie was taken care of.

On my way out the door, I noticed that the latest issue of some trendy clothing catalogue that no one in my family ever ordered from was sitting on the kitchen counter. I stuffed it in my book bag. Then I hopped on my scooter and zoomed to school. Mr. Nelson was going to announce the Perfect World Collage winners at the morning assembly, and I wanted to get a good seat.

As soon as I got to the auditorium, I spotted Mr. Pingler and yanked the catalogue out of my book bag. "Hey, Mr. Pingler," I said as I trotted up to him, "I just happened to be looking through this catalogue, and I thought of you."

Mr. Pingler looked puzzled. "Huh?" he asked.

"Right here on page twenty-seven. Look at these leather pants and this T-shirt," I pointed out. "These would look great on you, Mr. Pingler."

"I don't think I'm the leather-pants type, Lindsey, but thanks for thinking of me," he said.

"Sure you are," I said, stuffing the catalogue into his hands. "You keep this and look through it later. There are some clothes in here that would look awesome on you."

I left Mr. Pingler thumbing through the catalogue and found April, who'd saved me a seat about three rows down and was waving her arms at me.

"I'm sure you're going to win, Lindsey," April said, squeezing my hand as I sat down next to her.

"Naw, I'm sure it'll be you," I said. But secretly, I hoped April was right.

Mr. Nelson made about a million announcements and gave a speech about food fights in the lunchroom before he finally got around to the Perfect World Collage contest. He started by announcing the kindergarten winner and then went on to the first and second grades. By the time he announced the thirdgrade winner, I was practically having a heart attack.

Then, at last, I heard him say, "And now, the fourth-grade winner of our collage contest is . . ." I got ready to stand up. ". . . Blair Kolinski."

I almost swallowed my tongue.

"Blair created a truly unique collage on the theme of family and friends," Mr. Nelson went on.

UNIQUE? Blair had cut out pictures of her mom and dad and Missy and pasted them inside big, pink hearts. She wrote "Love Is All You Need" across the top. How lame is that! It was worse than lame, in fact. It was . . . oh, it didn't matter what it was. I'd lost.

"No way!" hissed April. "Who judged this thing, Blair's mother?"

"I have to go to the bathroom," I sputtered. Tears were welling up in my eyes, and my nose was starting to run. I got up and ran from the auditorium.

I stayed in the bathroom for the rest of the assembly and then went back to class feeling like a flat tire. Blair made a dramatic entrance, waving her giant first-prize blue ribbon around so everyone could gawk.

She "accidentally" swung it right in front of my face as she passed my desk.

"Blair, you may take your seat now," Miss Kinney said. "You all did a lovely job on your collages, and you should be very proud of yourselves. We'll hang them up on the bulletin boards this week so that you may admire each other's hard work."

Miss Kinney started going over a math assignment next, but I didn't hear a word.

When the bell rang, I charged for the door. I didn't even wait for April, and I didn't have the heart to ride my scooter. I just left it in its case and stomped home on foot.

I kept my eyes down and counted cracks in the sidewalk. How could Blair possibly have won that contest? Was there no justice in the world? Obviously not. I figured I could get a little sympathy from Mom, at least, and maybe talk her into making brownies for me. But then I remembered that all she cared about lately was ETHAN'S STUPID BAR MITZVAH!

The only thing I was good for, apparently, was baby-sitting Uncle Bernie and decorating trash cans. Uncle Bernie was right—trash cans are trashy. I felt like a trash can. No, I felt worse than a trash can. I felt like a worm—a small, slimy, brown worm. In my head, I composed a little poem about my wormness:

> Worm, worm, I am a worm,
> I have no legs or wings.
> I slither, I slide,
> In the brown dirt I hide.
> Oh, what a very sad thing.

Not bad, I thought. Maybe I wasn't a complete failure, after all. Maybe I had a future as a great poet.

By the time I got to my block, I was so busy imagining myself accepting the Nobel Prize for literature that I didn't notice all the excitement in my front yard until I heard Ethan shouting, "Here comes our little criminal now!" I looked up and saw a cop car parked in our driveway. Mom was standing in the yard with a huge police officer. He looked like a refrigerator with arms, and he was writing in a little notepad, just like on the TV shows. Holy cow.

Mrs. Schumacher was standing in the yard, too. So were Mrs. Thompson and Uncle Bernie. Then it hit me. Ethan had said "our little criminal."

"Lindsey!" Mom yelled. "Get over here, NOW!"

I started wracking my brain for all of the possible bad stuff I could have done, but I was coming up blank. "What's going on?" I squeaked as I walked up the driveway.

"It was her!" Mrs. Schumacher said, pointing a knobby finger at me. "She did it."

"Did what? What did I do?" I asked.

"You little vandal," croaked Mrs. Schumacher.

"Don't you call my daughter names," shouted my mom, suddenly coming to my defense and putting her arm around me. The police officer raised his hands and told everyone to calm down.

"Are you Lindsey Bergman?" he asked me.

I nodded.

"Do you know that defacing private property is a crime, Miss Bergman?"

"No. I mean, yes. I mean, I know it is, but I didn't deface anything," I sputtered.

"You are so busted, Garbage Girl," Ethan whistled.

Garbage Girl? What was Ethan talking about?

Oh my gosh, the trash cans. "The trash cans! Are you mad about the trash cans?" I cried. "I didn't deface them, I FACED them! Happy faces! I put happy faces on them to make them look cheerful and friendly."

"Then you *did* do it?" my mom asked. Her eyes looked like they were going to pop out of her head. "I thought I recognized those stickers," she moaned. "Lindsey, how could you?"

I tried to explain, but no one would give me a chance. Mrs. Schumacher was squawking that I owed her forty dollars. Ethan was laughing uncontrollably (until Uncle Bernie whacked him on the head). And

Mrs. Thompson had one of those I-just-knew-it-was-Lindsey looks on her face.

Then, to make matters worse—as if they could possibly get worse—Josh arrived. When he found out I was in trouble, he looked positively gleeful. Great, the entire fourth-grade class would know about this before sunset.

The police officer wrote me a warning ticket, and he and Mom worked out something about buying replacement trash cans for Mrs. Schumacher, who gave me a triumphant sniff before marching back to her house. Mrs. Thompson told my mother that she understood about having "problem children" and that if my mom wanted any advice, she should just call.

I sat down on the front steps and started to cry. Mom sat down and started to cry, too.

Uncle Bernie dragged Ethan—who was still giggling—into the house.

"Lindsey, what are we going to do with you?" Mom said, sighing.

"Sell me to the gypsies?" I offered glumly. "Just don't take away my scooter again." I got down on my knees in front of her. "Please?" I begged.

"I'm not going to take away your scooter. But your allowance for the next month will go toward buying new trash cans. I also want you to go right upstairs and write an apology note to the neighbors," said Mom. "And it had better be a good one."

I thought of telling her about my collage defeat to get a little sympathy, but I decided she was too mad to be handing out sympathy at that moment. So I stomped up to my room to work on my apology.

Dear Neighbor,

It's me, Lindsey. I want to tell you that I'm very sorry about putting happy faces on your trash cans. I thought they would look really good, but I know I should have asked first. I promise I will never lay a hand on your trash cans again, not even

if the wind blows them into the street
and someone in a big truck is about to
run over them.

Of course, if you liked the stickers, I have
a few left over. I would be happy to put
them on for you. Just give me a call.

Very truly yours,
Lindsey Bergman

I thought the part about the wind and the truck
was a nice touch. It showed how serious I was. So I
printed a bunch of copies and went out with Mr. Tiny
to deliver them.

We weren't gone more than thirty minutes, but
that's all the time it took for Mom and Ethan to get
into their biggest bar-mitzvah-planning fight yet. You
would think we'd had enough excitement for one day,
but nope. Mom and Ethan were going nuts in the
living room. And it was all because of eggplant.

Now, my mom is pretty smart, but she's smart in a

weird way. She can tell you how many varieties of ivy there are in the Midwest, but she's not too good at picking out food for a bunch of thirteen-year-old boys.

"Are you crazy?" screamed Ethan as he hurled a sofa pillow across the room. "Eggplant? You ordered EGGPLANT for my bar mitzvah? No one will eat that stuff! It's disgusting!"

"It's just a side dish. I thought it would be unique!" shouted Mom. "You don't want to be like everybody else, do you?" (I could have told her that that's exactly what Ethan wanted, but no one asked me.) "So, I guess now would not be a good time to tell you about the mime," Mom said, flopping into a chair.

"No way," Ethan sputtered. "You didn't."

"He's supposed to be wonderful, Ethan. The Feinbergs used him for Ben's bar mitzvah, and they loved him."

"Ben Feinberg is a total freak, Mom. He wears Elmo T-shirts to school!" Ethan looked so upset that I almost felt sorry for him. He was all sweaty, and his ears were purple. I think I actually saw zits appearing on his chin as he spoke.

"It's not bad enough that I have to read the hardest Torah portion in the world and give some stupid speech about how it feels to become a man," he continued. "Gee, Mom, maybe we could just get the mime to act the whole thing out for me!" With that, he turned and stormed out the door.

Mom collapsed onto the couch. "Lindsey, he's right," she said. "Let's face it, I stink at party planning." She brought her knees to her chin and mumbled that she'd made a huge mess out of Ethan's bar mitzvah and that the family would never forgive her. Then she rocked back and forth a little and hung her head. "What on earth was I thinking?" Mom sighed. "Even *I* don't like eggplant."

"It's OK, Mom," I said, squeezing her hand. But I was worried. My mother, the woman who stood on a chair at the last PTA meeting to protest cutbacks in art classes, was curled up in a little ball on the couch.

I poked her a couple of times, but she didn't move. "Do you want your fuzzy bunny slippers?" I asked.

"That won't help," she groaned. "What am I going to do? I've already paid the deposits for the mime and the special menu. It's too late to change things now."

I told her that it was never too late to fix a mess and that you just had to be creative. "And remember," I whispered, "Bergmans never quit."

Mom stayed in a ball. I sat on the couch and whistled patiently. Finally, she nodded and uncurled herself. "Let's get creative," she sighed.

I knew she'd come around. Bergmans always do.

I helped her figure out what to say to the mime and the catering lady. They were both very understanding when my mom explained that her son was highly allergic to eggplant and that I was terrified of mimes. (OK, so we lied, but nobody's feelings got hurt.) Then Mom called the banquet hall and ordered pizza and all-beef hot dogs for the kids, and stuffed chicken breast for the grownups.

There was still no entertainment, but we had time to work that out. I could always play my trumpet.

I was finishing my homework after dinner when Ethan finally came home. He'd been hiding out at his friend's house, feeling sorry for himself. When I told him I'd gotten Mom to change the menu and cancel the mime, he slugged me in the arm and said, "You're the best, creep. I guess I'll go practice my Hebrew."

Everyone seemed to be feeling much better. Dad's big project at work was almost over, and Mom was really relaxed. Uncle Bernie was the only one who wasn't looking perky. I could tell he was still thinking about Aunt Rhonda because, for a whole hour, he'd been writing her name over and over with one of my markers and then stabbing at the paper.

"Do you want to draw something with me, Uncle Bernie?" I offered.

"I'm not really in the mood, Pumpkin," he said.

"Come on, Uncle Bernie, you can't be feeling any

worse than I am. I almost got arrested today, and Blair Kolinski won the Perfect World Collage contest, and, well, I'm getting over it."

"You're right, honey. I should get over it, too," Uncle Bernie said, patting my hand. "I'm sorry about the collage," he added. "It was a dandy."

I shrugged. Then I got some more paper, and Uncle Bernie and I drew pictures of Blair Kolinski, Mrs. Schumacher, and Aunt Rhonda. We put snakes in their hair and gave them really big nostrils and no necks. It was very satisfying.

5

Rock Bottom

Two boring, uneventful weeks passed (highly unusual for me). Uncle Bernie went off cheese puffs and on a diet so he could impress Aunt Rhonda at the bar mitzvah. Ethan came home from school every day and practiced his Hebrew instead of picking on me or yelling at Mom. Things calmed down for Dad at work, so he was around to help Mom with bar mitzvah stuff—which made her a much happier person.

And I helped by making very cool skateboard-shaped place cards and decorating them with glow pens. Ethan liked the place cards so much that he punched my shoulder in gratitude.

We were just one big, happy family.

I was even starting to look forward to the bar mitzvah. Mostly because I couldn't wait to get Uncle Bernie and Cousin Sophie together.

Here's how I pictured it: Their eyes would meet across the buffet table. He'd pass her a cheese cube. She'd ask him if he wanted any pickled herring. The rest would be history.

Love was in the air. I could smell it. It was either love or the new I'm-about-to-be-a-man cologne that Ethan had started wearing. Whatever. It actually smelled good. And smelling it reminded me that I had to get cracking on my other romance project— Miss Kinney and Mr. Pingler.

When the bell rang for recess, I went up to Miss Kinney and said, "So, yesterday at band practice, a couple of us were telling Mr. Pingler how much we would all enjoy it if he came to our class and gave a little talk about jazz music. What do you think?"

Miss Kinney looked surprised, but she said, "Well,

I suppose it would be all right. Do you really think everyone would enjoy that?"

"Sure they would. He's a very inspiring speaker, and it might even make some of the kids want to take band next year." I smiled until my cheeks hurt.

"My, aren't you the little organizer," she said. "OK, I'll talk to Mr. Pingler."

I had to bite my lip to keep from squealing. I hated not telling her the whole truth, but I'm sure that Cupid would have done the same thing. "Thanks!" I shouted and ran to catch up with April.

On the playground, Missy and Blair were pelting April with the four-square ball. April was just standing there, looking miserable.

"Don't you two ever get tired of picking on people?" I asked as I grabbed the ball and threw it toward a flock of third graders.

"Well, if it isn't Super Dork to the rescue," said Blair.

"Yeah," said Missy.

"Can't you come up with anything more original

than *Super Dork?* No, of course you can't, because
you'd have to think about it for five minutes, and
you're too busy being obnoxious to think. Geez, you
guys are boring." I grabbed April's arm and headed
for the swings. Some of the kids on the playground
actually started clapping.

"Hey!" Blair yelled. "I am not boring! Nobody
calls me boring!"

"Yeah!" yelled Missy. But they both just stood
there, staring after us. Then Missy stuck out her leg
and tripped some little first grader who was chasing
a ball.

"I think they're getting tired of picking on me,"
said April.

"I think you're right. Hey, check it out," I said,
noticing that across the playground, Miss Kinney and
Mr. Pingler were having a deep discussion. "You
know, April, things just might be looking up for us."

I should have known better.

o

When I got home from school that afternoon, I found the front door wide open and the house dead quiet. I called around for Mom and Uncle Bernie, but no one answered. There were dishes in the sink, and the TV was cold—which meant that Uncle Bernie hadn't been around for a while. This was weird.

I was starting to get a little panicky when I heard a car pulling into the driveway. It was Dad. My dad never came home this early.

Someone must have died.

"Lindsey, honey," Dad said, coming through the door and throwing his arms around me.

"Who died?" I said.

"No one died. It's, well . . . it's Mr. Tiny. He's gone."

"What do you mean he's gone?" I yelped. "He lives here! Where did he go? Did somebody take him? Has he been kidnapped? Did you call the police?" I could hardly breathe.

Dad took my hand and sat down on the front steps with me. "Uncle Bernie took Mr. Tiny out for a walk this morning and, well, you know how Uncle Bernie always gets the leash caught around his legs?"

I nodded. I'd tried about a million times to show Uncle Bernie how to hold Mr. Tiny's leash, but he always messed it up and got all tangled.

Dad removed his glasses, wiped his eyes, and told me that Uncle Bernie let Mr. Tiny off the leash so he could untangle himself, and when he did, Mr. Tiny saw a squirrel and took off after it like a rocket. "Your mother and your uncle have been out looking for him all day." Dad pulled a tissue out of his pocket and blew his nose.

This was bad. Very bad. There were way too many awful things that could happen to a wiener dog who wasn't looking where he was going.

A giant lump rose in my throat, and my heart felt like a balloon being twisted into some weird animal shape by an angry clown.

"It's OK, Lindsey," Dad said, putting his arm around me. "We'll find him."

I burst into tears.

Then I ran into the house and called April. I told her to come right over and to bring a lot of tape. Next I called practically everyone in my neighborhood and told them to be on the lookout for the world's best wiener dog. Every time I felt like I was going to cry, I pinched my arm really hard.

Then I made up a flyer on Dad's computer and scanned in a great picture of Mr. Tiny at his birthday party last year.

I wanted to offer a five-hundred-dollar reward, but I had only twelve dollars and ninety-three cents. My scooter was worth a lot more than that. I'd miss the scooter, but I already missed Mr. Tiny even more.

As soon as April got to my house, we grabbed the flyer and headed out to the copy store. It took us awhile to get there, because I kept crying and had to stop to blow my nose a lot. I was sure that Mr. Tiny was scared and confused. And he hadn't had his late-afternoon chewy snack, so he was probably really hungry, too. Thinking about Mr. Tiny wandering around all alone in some strange place made me feel sick to my stomach.

But I had to pull myself together. My dog was counting on me.

We made twelve dollars and ninety-three cents' worth of copies, and then we went out and started taping the flyers up all over the neighborhood. We also put them in people's mailboxes and handed them to everyone we passed on the street.

By the time we got back to the house, we were exhausted, so Ethan took the rest of the flyers and went out on his bicycle. "Don't get used to me being nice, Lindsey. It'll probably never happen again," he said on his way out the door.

LOST!
Very handsome wiener dog
(also known as a dachshund)

Name: **Mr. Tiny**
Brown with **big**, warm eyes and a bald patch on his tummy.

Reward: Almost brand-new scooter with helmet. *Mint condition.*

Please call soon with information! **327-2**

I called the police, who were not very helpful at all. They said they didn't "do" missing dogs. I told them how special Mr. Tiny was, but they just said to call the animal shelter.

The people at the animal shelter said that since Mr. Tiny had tags, they'd be able to identify him and would call us if someone brought him in.

IF. So all we could do was wait. I hated waiting.

By dinnertime, Uncle Bernie and Mom still hadn't come back. April called her parents, and they said she could spend the night. Dad made us dinner, or something he thought was dinner, but mostly we just sat there and stared at it.

Mom and Uncle Bernie finally showed up at about eight-thirty. They'd been driving around all afternoon, and Uncle Bernie looked awful.

"Oh, Pumpkin," he said. "I'm so sorry. It's all my fault. I should never have let him off that leash. What was I thinking?" He slumped down on the couch and started pounding his fists on his head.

"It's OK," I said. "It could have happened to any-body." I was trying to be brave, but I could feel a knot forming in my throat. "I think April and I are going to bed now."

That night I dreamed I was a dog—a lost, scared dog—wandering through a long, dark alley lined with garbage cans. Suddenly they came to life and started chasing me. I ran as fast as I could, but I tripped and fell right into a big, ugly garbage can. The garbage can had a face. It was an evil, glow-in-the-dark monster face. I woke up all sweaty.

During Mr. Pingler's jazz lecture the next day, I tried to look interested. I had no idea what he was talking about, and I don't think anyone else did, either, because they all had their eyes closed.

At least Miss Kinney's eyes were open. Well, I think they were open. She had her hand over her face, so it was hard to tell. But the important thing was that Mr. Pingler was there, and he was wearing new leather pants! He was walking kind of funny in them, but I guess leather pants take some getting used to.

When he finished his talk, Miss Kinney, April, and I were the only ones clapping. Luckily, that woke up everyone else in the class, and then they clapped, too. Miss Kinney thanked Mr. Pingler and led him to the door, where they talked quietly for a minute. Maybe he was asking her for a date! He was looking at Miss Kinney with his eyes all big and round. It was the way Mr. Tiny looked at me when he wanted one of his special chewy snacks.

Everything, it seemed, reminded me of Mr. Tiny.

On the way home from school, April and I decided we should make a personal visit to the police station and the animal shelter. How could they refuse to help us if we were standing right there?

When we got to the police station, the officer at the front desk said he'd already told us they didn't "do" dogs. One of the other officers was a little nicer—he was the giant refrigerator-shaped man who had almost arrested me. He gave April and me a soda and told us to check with the animal shelter again. Then he asked me if I'd looked for Mr. Tiny in any trash cans. I think he thought he was making a little joke. It wasn't very funny.

We went to the animal shelter but didn't stay very long. It was too depressing to see all those cages filled with sad, homeless animals—especially since none of them was Mr. Tiny. So there was nothing left to do but go home.

Back at my house, April had a brilliant idea. She suggested we call the local television stations. "Maybe they'd do a special segment on Mr. Tiny!" she said. She really was the greatest friend in the whole world.

But the TV people told us that Mr. Tiny wasn't newsworthy.

The next day after school, April and I stopped by the shelter again, just in case. The only dog that had come in was a big, slobbery St. Bernard named Wilma. I was miserable.

To take my mind off things, I decided to try concentrating on Operation Pingler-Kinney. After my next band practice, I waited for everyone else to leave, and then I went up to Mr. Pingler.

"I probably shouldn't be telling you this," I started, "but I overheard Miss Kinney talking to Mrs. Andersen, you know, the librarian? Anyway, Miss Kinney was saying that she loved your jazz talk the other day and wished that you'd ask her out on a date so you could talk about music some more."

I waited for God to send a lightning bolt straight through me for fibbing again, but nothing happened.

"Lindsey," Mr. Pingler said with a chuckle. "I don't know what you think you heard, but . . ."

"Mr. Pingler, that's what I heard—I've got really good ears. I pinky-swear it."

"Pinky-swear," he repeated, rolling his eyeballs. "Is that so?" But a blush was starting to creep up his neck.

"Yeah, definitely. Well, I've gotta go now. I just thought you might want to know." I packed up my trumpet and started backing out the door. "Oh yeah, I almost forgot. She also told Mrs. Andersen that she loves tulips."

"I see. Well, thanks for the information, Lindsey."

After I left the room, I went to the window and peeked back inside. Mr. Pingler was grinning from ear to ear.

Ear to ear . . . Sigh. Mr. Tiny had the cutest, silkiest little ears in the world! I wanted my dog back and I wanted him now.

The next two days were torture. April and I went door-to-door again, asking all of the neighbors if they were SURE they hadn't seen Mr. Tiny. We made more flyers and gave them to store owners to hang in their windows. April's dad even drove us around in his Jeep. We called Mr. Tiny's name until we got hoarse. Then we came home and sucked on eucalyptus throat lozenges. I couldn't take much more of this.

○

It was day five without Mr. Tiny. I was drawing pictures of him in my notebook during recess when Blair marched up to me and said, "Hey, DORKFACE, Miss Kinney wants to see you back in the classroom, right now!"

"*Dorkface?* Oh yeah, that's *much* more original, Blair. I hope you didn't sprain your brain coming up with that one." Then her words sunk in.

Someone must have found Mr. Tiny! I pushed past Blair and ran faster than I'd ever run before, until I came puffing into the room all out of breath. "Where is he? Can I go pick him up? Who found him?" I was panting and gasping for air.

I thought I might faint, so I sat down in a chair to catch my breath. That's when I spotted the tulips.

They were beautiful. They were pink and white and yellow, and they were arranged in a pretty vase on Miss Kinney's desk.

Mr. Pingler had actually listened to me!

"Wow," I panted.

"Wow is right, Lindsey. As in, 'wow, are you in big trouble.' Do you have any idea what you've done?" she asked.

Uh-oh. "Don't you like them, Miss Kinney? I remember that once when we were studying spring, you said that tulips were your favorite flower—"

"Lindsey," she interrupted, "did you know that I'm engaged?"

"What?" I was stunned. "You can't be engaged! You don't wear a ring," I protested.

"Not everyone who's engaged wears a ring. I happen to be allergic to metals, so I can't wear one."

This was bad. No, this was beyond bad.

Miss Kinney went on. "Mr. Pingler is very upset and embarrassed. Apparently, he was led to believe that I might be interested in dating him. I explained to him as gently as possible that I was unavailable, but the entire incident was very humiliating for both of us."

"Miss Kinney, I'm sorry," I croaked. "I was sure that you two would be perfect for each other. I mean, Mr. Pingler wasn't eating lunch, and you were looking for someone sporty and romantic—"

"I know your intentions were good, Lindsey," she said. "But you had no business meddling in our personal lives. That's why they're called 'personal lives.' They're personal."

"I'm so sorry," I whispered again. I really meant it. Miss Kinney sat back in her chair and sighed. "I'm afraid that sorry is not enough to cover it this time, Lindsey. You will be on lunchtime cleanup duty for the next two weeks. And, right now, you will march down to the band room and apologize to Mr. Pingler."

Oh, great.

"And Lindsey," Miss Kinney said as I turned to leave, "I also called your mother."

After I apologized to Mr. Pingler (who was about as happy with me as Miss Kinney was), I spent the rest of the day at school not talking to anyone. I figured that if I didn't open my mouth, my mouth couldn't get me into any more trouble.

I had hit rock bottom. My life was a total disaster. And I didn't even have my dog to comfort me. Of course, if I'd had my dog, then my life wouldn't really be a disaster and I wouldn't need comforting, but—oh well, it didn't matter. I was a worm.

I slithered home. When I got there, Mom was waiting for me with a big lecture.

"When are you going to learn to mind your own business, Lindsey?" Mom scolded. "Not only is it *wrong* to meddle in people's love lives, but it can be very dangerous. It always leads to trouble."

She didn't need to convince me. I was never going to interfere again. From now on, no more matchmaking, no more trying to solve other people's problems, no more meddling—*ever.*

Suddenly, I had a very nervous feeling in my stomach. Maybe it hadn't been such a fantastic idea to send Cousin Sophie that invitation . . .

"Lindsey," Mom said. "Are you paying attention? You look like you're a million miles away."

That's probably where I should be, I thought glumly. A million miles away. My family could put me in a box and ship me to the South Pole. There was no way I could ruin anything down there.

Then I remembered about penguins. They live at the South Pole and, knowing me, I'd probably start some big fight between two formerly peaceful flocks of penguins and it would turn into a giant penguin war and . . . I couldn't bear to think about it.

6

Forgiveness

I woke up all sweaty and shaking from a night-mare about giant, penguin-eating tulips.

I was clutching my pillow (which I thought was a penguin) and trying to save it from a nasty, sharp-toothed tulip that I had just kicked in the stem. I'd actually kicked over my lamp, and the thump of it hitting the floor woke me up.

It was Saturday, but who cared? It might as well be a Wednesday. Mr. Tiny was still missing, and April had gone to visit her grandmother for the weekend. I figured I'd just stay in bed all day and pout.

Suddenly I heard more thumping. I looked at my lamp, and it wasn't moving. But something was going on downstairs. There was yelling and stomping, and a door slammed, and my dad called, "Lindsey! Lindsey! Come quick!" The last time he yelled like that, there was a solar eclipse that he wanted me to see.

"Lindsey, hurry!" It was Mom this time.

I climbed out of bed and padded downstairs. Mom, Dad, Ethan, and Uncle Bernie were all huddled around the front door. In the middle of them was Josh Thompson, and he was holding Mr. Tiny!

"MR. TINY!" I cried. He leaped out of Josh's arms and into mine. He was wiggling all over, wagging his tail and licking my face. "Where did you find him?"

"I was doing my paper route on the other side of town this morning," Josh answered cooly, "and I saw him digging in someone's yard. I was pretty sure it was your dog. But I checked his stomach, just to make sure."

"Really? Thanks," I managed to squeak out between Mr. Tiny's licks. "But I thought you hated me. Why'd you save my dog?"

Josh turned kind of red. "I don't hate you, Lindsey. You're a girl, and you're my neighbor. I'm supposed to pick on you."

That made sense. So Mom asked Josh if he wanted to stay for pancakes.

After pancakes, we gave Mr. Tiny a bath, because he was kind of stinky from his travels. Then we took him for a walk (WITH HIS LEASH). And I discovered that Josh really wasn't so bad for a boy.

I even asked Mom if I could invite him to Ethan's bar mitzvah, which was only a week away. Josh didn't know much about bar mitzvahs, so I told him all about them, including the fights over the invitations and the food and the entertainment. Then he told me that his cousin played guitar for the Twisted Turtles and that they'd probably play at the bar mitzvah for free since we were such close family friends!

Ethan was so excited when he found out about the Twisted Turtles that he jumped onto the dining-room table and started playing air guitar. Dad suggested we might want to purchase earplugs for the older guests.

Everyone was getting excited. Mom got a new haircut and had her nails done. I wanted mine done, too, but Mom said that manicures were too expensive for ten-year-old girls. So Uncle Bernie gave me a French manicure with white enamel and clear nail polish. It looked so good that April had him paint hers, too.

Dad started to call our house Bar Mitzvah Central. Relatives kept phoning to see if they could bring things like chopped liver or pickled herring. I asked Mom if they were trying to poison us. "Couldn't they bring normal stuff, like cookies or potato chips?"

Uncle Bernie was doing sit-ups every morning and trying to decide which splashy tie to wear to make ex-Aunt Rhonda jealous. I almost told him about inviting Cousin Sophie, but I decided that what he didn't know couldn't hurt him. And anyway, who knew? Maybe they would actually hit it off. He might look so cute, she wouldn't be able to resist him.

With twenty-four hours to go, everything was looking great.

Then Ethan got weird. It happened while Mom was hemming his suit pants. He was looking at himself in the mirror and watching my mother crawl around the floor at his ankles, when he suddenly blurted out, "I'm not doing it."

Then my brother took off his pants, walked into his room, and locked the door.

"Oh dear," said Mom. "He's got the jitters."

"He'll be fine," said Dad. "As I recall, I felt the same way before my bar mitzvah."

"You threw up before your bar mitzvah," Uncle Bernie chimed in.

"Thanks for reminding me," said Dad.

"Don't mention it, Gordy."

Ethan didn't come out of his bedroom for the rest of the night. Mom sat outside the door for a while and tried to talk to him. So did Dad and Uncle Bernie. But Ethan wasn't budging. I went to bed.

The next morning I woke up to the smell of toast and coffee and the sound of Mr. Tiny snoring in my ear. "It's bar mitzvah day, Mr. Tiny," I said softly. His tail went thump, thump, thump.

I put on my robe and went downstairs. There were Mom, Dad, Uncle Bernie . . . and no Ethan.

"We'll give him until eight o'clock, and then we take the hinges off the door," said Dad, refilling his coffee cup.

"Honey, I don't think that's the way we want to handle it," Mom said. "I'm sure he'll be down in a minute."

At eight o'clock sharp, Dad went to get the screwdriver. We all stood outside Ethan's door.

"Son, if you don't come out, we're coming in!" shouted Dad. He counted to twenty. The door didn't open. "Back away from the door, Ethan! We've had enough of this nonsense." He picked up the screwdriver and went after the hinges.

"I want Lindsey," came Ethan's voice from behind the door.

No way, I thought. He must have just said something that *rhymed* with Lindsey.

"Lindsey can come in, but nobody else. Understand?" came Ethan's voice again.

"Whatever you say, dear," said Mom, and she shoved me toward the door.

"Uh-uh!" I protested. I was not going to get into the middle of this one. I'd made a promise to myself, and I was sticking to it. "I am SO not going through that door. Every time I try to help out, it turns into a disaster. You can find yourselves another meddler."

They all stood there, stunned. I turned on one heel and marched off to my room.

Uncle Bernie came trotting after me.

"Pumpkin," he pleaded. "This is no time to take a stand. We need your—"

"Forget it, I'm not getting involved." I tossed my hair back and crossed my arms over my chest. I was holding firm on this one.

"This is not the Lindsey I know," Uncle Bernie said. "The Lindsey I know would do anything to help her family."

"Yeah, well, that was before I learned my lesson. Meddling in other people's problems just ends up getting you into trouble."

"Lindsey." Uncle Bernie tipped my chin so I had no choice but to look him straight in the eye. "This isn't meddling. Your brother is *asking* for your help," he said. "There's a very big difference between that and you deciding to talk your band teacher into wearing leather pants."

I couldn't help it—I had to laugh.

I thought about it for a moment. "I guess you're

right, Uncle Bernie . . . OK, I'll give it a shot."

Of course, this also meant I was going to have to go into that black hole that Ethan called a bedroom. Gross. I stood outside his room and knocked softly. "Ethan, it's me," I said.

He unlocked the door and opened it a crack. I squeezed through.

Ethan's room smelled like old cheese, and there were clothes and candy-bar wrappers and motorcycle magazines all over the floor.

I was glad I was a girl.

"I can't do it, Lindsey," Ethan said. He was sitting on top of his unmade bed, clutching a pillow. "I just know I'm going to screw up and embarrass myself. I'm going to get up there and do something stupid, like forget my Hebrew, or drop the Torah, or trip the rabbi—I just know it."

"No way, Ethan. You've been practicing for months," I pointed out. "Your Hebrew is fine, and you're very coordinated."

"But I'm not brave like you, Lindsey. I can't stand the thought of messing up in front of everybody. You mess up all the time and don't care, but I'm not like that. I don't like risks."

Now, I didn't think I messed up *all* the time, but I guessed I understood what he meant. "Hey, you're really good at risks, too," I coaxed. "Remember when you asked Natalie Winkie to the sixth-grade dance, and she laughed at you?"

"So, what's your point, Lindsey?" Ethan snapped.

I reminded him that he'd asked four other girls before Sydney Alexander had finally said yes. "And you and Sydney won the dance contest," I said. "If you'd given up when Natalie said no—"

"OK, I get it," Ethan said. "But this is different. This is bigger."

I pointed out that he was bigger, too. "You can do this, Ethan. I know you can. You're a Bergman. Besides having slightly webbed toes, we Bergmans have guts. Use your guts."

Ethan nodded, smiled, and slugged me in the arm.
I slugged him back.

Ethan was amazing at his bar mitzvah, and I got
all goose-bumpy watching him. Mom and Dad cried,
and Uncle Bernie's nose dripped a lot. Ethan was
actually glowing. (Well, maybe he was just sweaty.)

At the banquet hall afterward, April and I helped
everyone find their seats. Ex-Aunt Rhonda made a
grand entrance with her new boyfriend (who looked
like a tree stump), and April showed them to a table
as far away from Uncle Bernie's as possible.

Then Cousin Sophie arrived. She looked even
prettier than I remembered. "I'll take this one," I whispered to April.

Ignoring the nervous feeling in my stomach, I said
hello to Cousin Sophie and showed her to a seat at
Uncle Bernie's table. He was in the buffet line loading
up his plate, and he'd left his jacket draped over his
chair. I made sure not to put Sophie right next to him,

since that would definitely have fallen into the "meddling" category. But I figured across the table from him was perfectly safe.

"Where are your parents, Lindsey?" Sophie asked. "I'd like to thank them for having me. You know, with everything that's happened, I really wasn't expecting to be invited."

I had no idea what she was talking about, and I wasn't really sure I wanted to know. I pointed out my parents and then left to catch up with April in the buffet line.

I had just helped myself to some potato salad when the yelling started.

"You should have minded your own business, you two-faced, back-stabbing busybody. You ruined my life!" Uncle Bernie shouted.

"You ruined your own life, you lazy slob!" Cousin Sophie shot back.

Uh-oh.

Mom came running up, with Dad right behind

her. "What's SHE doing here?" Mom asked. "She wasn't on the list!"

Dad shrugged helplessly.

I chewed nervously on my lip. "Um, why wasn't she on the list?" I asked. I could feel my face turning hot and red.

"Because she's the one who talked Aunt Rhonda into leaving Uncle Bernie," Mom hissed.

I felt like my head was going to explode.

"Lindsey," Dad said, turning slowly to me. "Did you have something to do with this?"

I gulped. "Well, sort of, maybe a little . . . yes."

There was nothing left to do but confess. I told my parents everything.

Meanwhile, Cousin Sophie and Uncle Bernie were having a full-blown food fight, launching their dinners at each other. People started ducking under tables. And that's when the matzo ball came flying through the air and hit me—*splat!*—in the face.

Finally, two of my braver uncles jumped in and

pulled Uncle Bernie and Cousin Sophie away from each other. Things got very quiet. Dad handed me a napkin to wipe my face. Sophie picked up her purse, pulled a radish out of her hair, and left the banquet hall. Uncle Bernie marched into the men's room.

I had really done it this time. I was truly a worm. I started to cry.

April came up to me and whispered in my ear, "Don't cry. Fix it."

"But how?" I blubbered. "It's too late!"

"Come on," she said, dragging me toward the men's room. "You can start with Uncle Bernie."

I had never been in a men's room before (and I don't plan on ever going in one again). Uncle Bernie was standing at the mirror, wiping off his new tie.

"I'm so sorry, Uncle Bernie," I sputtered. "I did a stupid, terrible thing. And I promise, if you'll forgive me, I'll never do anything this stupid or terrible again." I took a paper towel and blew my nose. "I only did it because I love you," I sniffled.

Uncle Bernie looked at me. "Pumpkin, how could this have been your fault?"

I told him the whole story about trying to set him up with Sophie. He stared at me for a minute. (It was a very long minute.) Then he started laughing. He laughed until I thought he was going to hurt himself.

"Well, you certainly did learn your lesson, didn't you?" he snorted, handing me another paper towel. "Don't worry, I forgive you. And don't tell anyone, but I've been dying to throw something at that woman for months! Now, come here and give me a hug."

If everyone had an Uncle Bernie, I thought, the world would be a better place. I squeezed him for all I was worth.

"Um, Uncle Bernie, could we get out of this bathroom now?" I asked.

"Sure, but only on one condition," he said.

"Anything you want."

"Dance with me!"

Oh geez.

By the time we came out of the bathroom, the caterers had just about finished cleaning up the mess from the food fight. I found Mom and Dad and Ethan and apologized from the bottom of my meddling heart. Then the Twisted Turtles started playing, and Uncle Bernie whipped me out onto the dance floor.

We did a wild, thrashy, completely embarrassing dance, and everybody clapped. Pretty soon, April and Josh and Mom and Dad joined in. We all twirled and jumped like one big, crazy tornado.

Later, while we were taking a punch break, Uncle Bernie leaned over and said, "Take a look around the room, Lindsey."

I looked. Mom and Dad were dancing together. Ethan was impressing some eighth-grade girls with his air guitar. And April and Josh were eating cookies and watching the band.

"I see a lot of happy faces, Pumpkin. And a lot of them are happy because of you," said Uncle Bernie.

"I don't know. I still feel pretty much like a worm."

"Worm, schmerm!" Uncle Bernie hooted. "You're more like a butterfly. Sometimes you flit before you think, but you make the people around you feel light and sunny. Especially me. And believe me, it's not easy to make me feel light and sunny."

I thought about that for a minute. I gazed up at him. Maybe it was the splashy tie, but he did look a lot better than he had that first day on our couch.

Suddenly, I felt like flitting. I grabbed Uncle Bernie's hand and headed for the dance floor.

True Stories

Meet three American girls who, like Lindsey, try their best to make the world a better place—and stick to it, even when the going gets tough!

Hilary Staver

loves tigers. When she learned there were only 6,000 of these beautiful, endangered cats left in the wild, she had to act—especially since her school mascot is the tiger. So she put up a poster, explaining the animals' plight. "Tigers are hunted illegally because some people think parts of the tiger have healing powers," says Hilary, who raised $500 for the tigers' protection and wrote to the World Wildlife Fund for more information. Months later, all she had received was a fact sheet about tigers.

But Hilary didn't give up. When she was interviewed by her local paper, the World Wildlife Fund finally took notice and invited her to meet the president, the head of wildlife programs, and the tiger specialist. "They were great," says Hilary, who continues to make an impact by teaching people about tigers.

And she's already moved on to her next project—starting a recycling program at her school!

go tigers!

One day, Brita Thomas noticed that her class-mate had to sit out of gym class because she didn't have shoes. Brita used allowance money to buy her friend a pair, but soon Brita learned there were many other children in her Minnesota community in the same situation. So with the help of her family and her 4-H group, she started Happy Feet, a program that provides gym shoes to kids in need. By writing letters to companies and organizations and taking donations from private citizens, Brita and her volunteers have raised enough money to buy shoes for over 5,000 kids!

Shopping for shoes is the fun part. What isn't as easy, says Brita, is getting some people to believe that not every-one can afford something as simple as gym shoes. But after Brita and her friends appeared on TV and radio shows, "that helped people realize that what we were doing was important," she says. "They started taking us seriously."

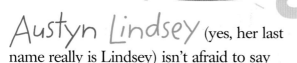

Austyn Lindsey (yes, her last name really is Lindsey) isn't afraid to say "Slow down!" When she and her Girl Scout troop learned that manatees, Florida's beloved marine mammals, were being wounded and sometimes killed by boats speeding through shallow water, Austyn and her troop jumped in. They donated earnings from cookie sales to groups that protect manatees, and they wrote letters to Florida's governor and senators and the U.S. Fish and Wildlife Commission. They even wrote and performed a song on the radio!

But it isn't always easy to get results. After Austyn and her troop saw manatees at a local beach—many with scars from boat-propeller cuts—the girls asked authorities to declare the beach a "No Wake" zone and to post a speed-limit sign for boaters. But a year later, Austyn's troop saw more manatees and no sign!

"We're not giving up," says Austyn. She knows that change comes slowly.

Meet the Author

Although Chryssa Atkinson has never been hit with a matzo ball, she has always secretly wanted to throw one. She spent much of her childhood trying to explain why she shouldn't get in trouble for brilliant schemes that didn't work out the way she thought they would. Today, she lives near Chicago with her very patient husband, two silly children, and the world's hairiest dog.

Visit americangirl.com
and click on **Fun for Girls**
for quizzes and games.

Place
Stamp
Here

☆ American Girl™

PO BOX 620497
MIDDLETON WI 53562-0497